Published by Crown Publishers, Inc., One Park Avenue, New York, N.Y. 10016 and simultaneously in Canada by General Publishing Company Limited. Manufactured in Hong Kong.

Library of Congress Cataloging in Publication Data. Gantz, David. The O'Hare family in—the seasons. Summary: The O'Hare family enjoy different activities in each season of the year. (1. Seasons—Fiction. 2. Rabbits—Fiction) I. Title. II. Title: The seasons. PZ7. G15350hat 1984 (E) 84–3239 ISBN 0-517-55460-7

First Edition

10   9   8   7   6   5   4   3   2   1

THE O'HARE FAMILY IN
The Seasons

by
David
Gantz.

CROWN PUBLISHERS, INC. NEW YORK

—SPRING—

"It's the day before Easter," said Papa, Harmony O'Hare. "Mama, we're going on a picnic."

"May I bring my kite?" asked Three O'Hare.

"Of course you may," replied Mama, Melody O'Hare.

"I'm taking my sailboat," said Two O'Hare.
"I'm taking my fishing rod," said One O'Hare.
"And I'm taking my guitar," said Papa O'Hare.
Mama packed a picnic lunch, and they all piled
into the family car and drove off.

There was a sweet smell of spring in the air.
"Look!" said Papa. "See the insects pollinating
the flowers—and there's Mrs. Beaver hanging out
her wash to dry in the warm wind."
"Wave hello to Farmer Brown Bear," said Mama.
Farmer Brown Bear was driving his tractor.

"What's he doing?" asked Two O'Hare.

"He's plowing his fields to make them ready for spring planting," replied Papa O'Hare.

"Careful Papa," said Mama. "There's Harriet
Hen and her new Easter chicks out for a walk."
"Don't worry, I see them," Papa replied.

"Look, there's a perfect spot for our picnic," said
Mama, pointing to a big sheltering oak tree on top
of a little hill.

    While Mama spread out the picnic lunch, Papa
played some tunes on his guitar.
    Three O'Hare flew his kite in the brisk breeze.

One and Two O'Hare found a little brook where
Two O'Hare sailed her boat and One O'Hare did
some fishing.

Before packing up to go home, the children picked some blue crocus, white narcissus, red tulips, purple violets, and yellow daffodils.

When they got home, Mama boiled the eggs she bought from Farmer Brown Bear. Then One, Two, and Three O'Hare got out their paints and decorated the eggs for Easter.

—SUMMER—

It was the Fourth of July and the O'Hares decided to spend the day at the beach. Papa loaded the beach chairs, blanket, beach umbrella, and his guitar into the car. Mama took her knitting, and One, Two, and Three O'Hare took their pails and shovels.

When they got to the beach, Papa set up the
beach umbrella and chairs. Then he sat down and
read his newspaper while Mama O'Hare worked
on her knitting.

"May we go in the water?" asked Two O'Hare. "Yes," replied Mama, "but be sure to stay where the lifeguard can see you."

One, Two, and Three O'Hare ran off to play in the waves and watch the snorklers and surfers. After a while, they settled down to build sand castles in front of the lifeguard stand.

At lunchtime Papa took them to the refreshment
stand where they had frankfurters and orange drinks.

When nighttime came they watched a dazzling
display of fireworks from the boardwalk.

On the way home, One, Two, and Three O'Hare
fell asleep after their exhausting but fun-filled day.

—FALL—

"Halloween and Thanksgiving will soon be here," said Papa. "Hop into the car everybody. We're going out to Farmer Brown Bear's."

"What for?" asked Two O'Hare.

"To buy some pumpkins," replied Mama.

The brightly colored leaves of red, yellow, and
brown swirled all around them as Papa drove the
car out to the farm.

Farmer Brown Bear was busy stacking cornhusks. Mrs. Brown Bear was bringing in a load of freshly harvested pumpkins. The farmhands were picking ripe apples and pears from the fruit trees.

Papa O'Hare bought a pumpkin for each of the children.

When they got home, Mama showed the children how to carve faces into the pumpkins. Papa put a candle inside each pumpkin and, at bedtime, lit them. One, Two, and Three O'Hare watched the pumpkins glow as they fell asleep.

—WINTER—

On the night before Christmas, One, Two, and Three O'Hare wished for snow before they went to sleep.

When they awoke the next morning, Christmas day, everything was covered with a blanket of fresh, white snow.

The family gathered around the Christmas tree and opened their presents. Papa got a new set of skis, and Mama, a beautiful woolen scarf and hat.

One O'Hare got a new sled, Two O'Hare got ice skates, and Three O'Hare got snowshoes.

The whole family dressed warmly, and they all went out to play in the snow.

Papa tried his new skis on the hill and One O'Hare followed on his new sled.

Two O'Hare tried her skates on the frozen pond, and Mama helped Three O'Hare walk on the soft snow with his new snowshoes.

After a while they all got together and built a
snowman using Mama's old scarf and one of Papa's
old hats.

Toward the end of the day they built snow forts
and had a friendly snowball fight.

When they were all wet and tired, they went back into the house.

Papa built a fire and Mama made hot chocolate for everybody.